The Haunted House & Flight to Nowhere

Merry Christmas, Kelly!
Our Love,
Larry & Cheryl

Two stories based on the Universal Television Series
HARDY BOYS™/NANCY DREW™
Mysteries

The Haunted House
Flight to Nowhere

By Michael Sloan

By James Henerson

Novelizations by Stratemeyer Syndicate

The Haunted House
By Stratemeyer Syndicate
Based on the Universal Television Series
HARDY BOYS™/NANCY DREW™ MYSTERIES
Developed for Television by Glen A. Larson
Based on the HARDY BOYS™ books by Franklin W. Dixon
Adapted from the episode THE HOUSE ON POSSESSED HILL
Written by Michael Sloan

Flight to Nowhere
By Stratemeyer Syndicate
Based on the Universal Television Series
HARDY BOYS™/NANCY DREW™ Mysteries
Developed for Television by Glen A. Larson
Based on the HARDY BOYS books by Franklin W. Dixon
Adapted from the episode THE FLICKERING TORCH MYSTERY
Written by James Henerson

Grosset & Dunlap
A Filmways Company
Publishers · New York

Library of Congress Catalog Card Number: 78-52858
ISBN: 0-448-16197-4

Published simultaneously in Canada
Printed in the United States of America

CONTENTS

The Haunted House

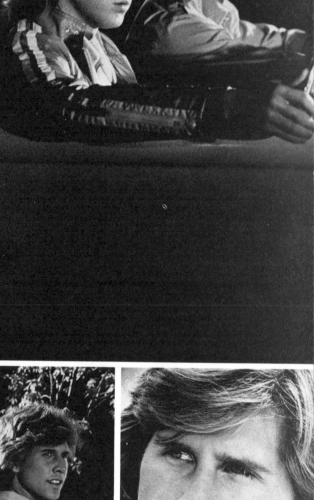

*D*usk had fallen and street lights illuminated the gloomy façade of the Blackhawk Hotel in downtown Emmetville. Few people were walking the streets, and traffic was slow.

Frank Hardy and his younger brother, Joe, were sitting on a pair of small street-licensed trail bikes some distance from the hotel, balancing their cycles with their feet. They watched a handsome man in his late forties come out of the hotel and walk briskly toward a parked car.

"Now what do you have to say?" asked Joe. He was seventeen years old.

"I see it, but I don't believe it!" Frank muttered as the man started the car and drove off. "Even if he lied to us," he went on, "I don't feel right, following my own father."

"Doesn't seem to bother him," Joe replied philosophically.

Just then the boys noticed another man, who jumped into a car and began to tail Mr. Hardy. Frank and Joe looked at each other and fired up their bikes.

"Something's going on, Joe!" Frank said tensely.

"One thing is sure," his brother added. "Dad isn't on a fishing trip!"

"Joe, I think he's in some kind of trouble. I can feel it!"

The Hardys gave the second car a safe head start, then set out after it. The chase led through the midtown area onto a highway. After a few miles they turned into a side road. Then, to the great surprise of the boys, Fenton Hardy drove into the Emmetville cemetery. His shadow stopped outside the large gate.

Frank slowed his bike. "We may have to follow them on foot!" he called to his brother.

"Follow them where? You don't mean in there?"

"You know a better way to find out what's going on?"

"I'm not so sure I want to know what's going on in a cemetery," Joe replied lamely.

The stranger parked beside the entrance and got out of his car. He was a large, well-groomed man. Silently he went up to the gate and peered at the manicured, rolling green lawn, dotted with monuments.

Frank and Joe concealed their bikes in a cluster of trees. The older boy dismounted and stashed his helmet on the back of his cycle, shaking out his hair.

"What's he doing?" Joe asked.

"I don't know, but we'd better tip Dad."

"Frank, what if we're wrong about that guy? He may be visiting somebody — a relative!"

"He's visiting a relative, all right. Ours!"

Reluctantly Joe climbed off his bike and followed

Frank toward the entrance. It was quite dark now, with only a sliver of moonlight illuminating the tombstones. An eerie bird call pierced the stillness as the boys slipped through the gate.

They saw the vague outline of their father and that of his shadow ahead of them. Mr. Hardy seemed to be searching for a particular area in the cemetery. He consulted a piece of paper in his hand, then walked up a knoll and stopped. His shadow ducked, and the boys pressed close to a large marble cross.

The detective bent over to read the name on a tombstone, then took a notebook from his coat pocket and wrote it down.

"To think we could be watching Monday-night football," Joe whispered to his brother. "What's he doing now?"

"The same thing we are. Sneaking around a cemetery in the dark."

Fenton Hardy put the notebook back in his pocket and turned to leave. His shadow retreated silently between the trees, and the boys hurried to the gate. As they passed the stranger's car, Joe stopped and reached through the open window.

"Joe, are you crazy?" Frank hissed. "He's right behind us."

Joe did not reply. Instead, he grabbed a box of cough drops from the dashboard.

Frank shook his head in disbelief. "This is a fine time to be stealing cough drops!"

"I'm not stealing cough drops. I'm lifting a fingerprint," Joe explained and carefully removed the cellophane from the box. Then he tossed the cough drops back on the dash and the boys ran toward the trees where they had parked their bikes.

It was none too soon. The stranger hurried through the gate and climbed into his car. Seconds later, Mr. Hardy drove out of the cemetery and sped past the boys without noticing them.

Joe kicked over his cycle and raced the engine. "We've got to warn him!"

"We've got to think before we move," Frank cautioned. "Dad didn't tell us he was working on a case for a reason. We could stumble in and mess up something very important."

"But Dad doesn't know he's being followed!"

"How do we know that? Dad was one of New York City's best cops for twenty years."

"So what do we do?"

"We get back to the office and find out everything we can about this case." Frank gunned his bike and they disappeared into the darkness.

They drove straight home, parked their cycles in the driveway, and hurried into the house. Aunt Gertrude, their father's unmarried sister, who lived with them, poked her head out of the kitchen. "How come you boys are never in time for dinner?"

"You heard from Dad?" Frank asked, ignoring her question.

"Now why would I have heard from him? He's on a fishing trip."

Frank and Joe looked at each other. "We'd better

check the office. See if Callie heard anything," Frank said. Callie was Mr. Hardy's part-time secretary, and a good friend of the boys.

They turned without further comment, but Aunt Gertrude knew something was up. She grabbed Joe by the arm. "Your brother has that look!" she declared. "What's wrong?"

"I don't know what's wrong, Aunt Gertrude," Joe mumbled and pulled loose. "That's the truth."

Aunt Gertrude shook her head and stood quietly for a moment, then went back into the kitchen.

Frank and Joe hurried to their father's office, which was located next to the garage. In the front room, a pretty, energetic girl of Frank's age was still busy at her desk. She looked up in surprise when the boys rushed in.

Frank questioned her about his father's whereabouts. "Callie, he must have said something!" the boy urged. "Even if it didn't seem important at the time, try to remember."

Callie smiled. "If it didn't seem important at the time, why would I remember?"

"Joe, we're just going to have to level with her. Tell her what's going on."

"What is going on?" Joe asked.

"Yes, what is going on?" Callie repeated.

"We don't know," Frank admitted.

Callie still smiled. "Fascinating."

"Callie, have you noticed how Dad's been acting very suspicious and secretive?" Frank asked.

"Since when is a fishing trip suspicious?"

13

"Since he didn't take his fishing gear with him," Joe answered.

"We saw him a few hours ago over in Emmetville," Frank stated.

"You're mistaken. I made reservations for him at the lake."

Joe looked straight into Callie's eyes. "Herbie Stahlmaster saw Dad at the county seat yesterday morning. He was coming out of the Blackhawk Hotel."

"We called and Dad was registered," Frank added. "We went over there —"

"Well," Callie interrupted, "there has to be a reason, and it's obviously not our business. At least it's not mine. I've finished the letters your father left for me and I'd like to lock up and go home."

"We'll lock up," Frank offered. "We want to look around."

Callie pushed back her chair and stood up. "I'm holding you both responsible for the condition of this office when your father gets back!" she warned.

The boys nodded as she walked out the door.

"She's right," Joe said. "We have no right to pry into Dad's cases when we aren't asked."

"I think he was afraid of involving us and now we know he could be in real danger." Frank rifled through the roladex on his father's desk, then picked up the phone. He dialed a number. "Mr. Hardy's room, please."

"What are you doing?" Joe asked. "He's going to

kill us when he finds out we were following him!"

"I don't think so," Frank said. "Not when we tell him about the man we saw on his tail."

He listened a moment, then spoke into the mouthpiece again. "Are you sure? I know he was registered there this morning. . . . When was that? . . . Thank you." He hung up.

"What is it?" Joe asked.

"He checked out an hour ago."

"That's that. He's probably on his way home to tell us all about the case. We won't even have to admit we were spying on him."

"We weren't spying on him."

"What were we doing?"

"Maintaining precautionary surveillance."

Joe chuckled. "I hope he appreciates the difference."

"At least I feel better," Frank said. "If he was able to check out of the hotel, he must be all right." He began to look through a mountain of correspondence in their father's office, while Joe went to the lab to work on the cellophane wrapper from the box of cough drops he had taken from the stranger's car.

He returned about half an hour later with a slide and a microscope.

Frank, who had been studying his father's latest correspondence, threw up his hands in despair. "There are just too many possibilities," he declared. "I can't find a case that stands out."

"But I've got a beauty that stands out," Joe said and set up the microscope on the desk.

Frank looked over his brother's shoulder as he put in the slide. "Looks like a thumb print," he said.

The young sleuths studied it closely, not knowing what to do next. Just then Aunt Gertrude walked into the office. "Boys, it's almost eleven!"

"I'm finished here," Joe said.

"First thing in the morning we'll try to retrace all of Dad's known movements," Frank decided.

"What for?" Aunt Gertrude wanted to know. "Your father will be back from his fishing trip in the morning."

Joe got up and started to walk out of the room. "I can't wait to see what he's caught!"

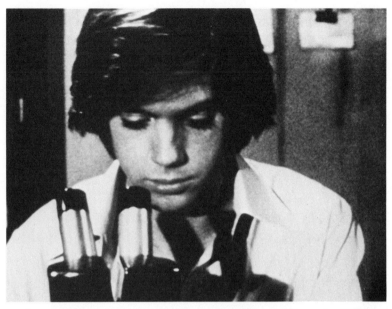

Aunt Gertrude looked curiously at Frank. "What is it that you two aren't telling me?"

"There's nothing to tell, Aunt Gertrude. We're just anxious to see Dad, that's all."

Miss Hardy followed the boys out of the office with an apprehensive look on her face. If she had known of the situation her brother found himself in at this point, she would have been extremely upset.

The detective had been well aware of his shadow en route to Emmetsville. After he left the cemetery, he did not head back to the highway, but instead drove along a narrow, deserted road at high speed for several miles. Then he pulled to the side, concealed his car as well as he could, and turned off the lights.

Seconds later his shadow sped past, unaware that now *he* was the one who was being watched.

Mr. Hardy smiled grimly, started his engine, and headed in the opposite direction. But soon a car spun out of nowhere and blocked the road. The detective skidded to a halt, went into reverse gear, and tried to back away. However, when he looked in the rearview mirror, he saw his former shadow round the corner and drive up behind him. He was trapped!

He slammed on the brakes and was about to wheel hard to his right when a man appeared at his window. "I wouldn't!" the stranger warned.

Mr. Hardy stared at him. A shoulder holster protruded from the man's jacket. To make matters worse, the detective's former shadow climbed out of his car and approached from the other side.

"Out, Mr. Hardy!" the stranger with the gun commanded. "Right now!"

The detective had no choice. Slowly he obeyed. "Who are you?" he asked, while the stranger politely held the door for him.

"All in due time, Mr. Hardy," was the clipped answer. "All in due time."

The two men hustled the detective into his shadow's car and drove to a residential area of town, where they pulled up in front of a one-family house.

"Out, Mr. Hardy!" his shadow commanded.

"Look fellows, hasn't this gone far enough?"

The men stared at him coldly and opened the

doors. Mr. Hardy realized that there was no use in defying their orders. He smiled grimly and got up. "Thanks."

They led him into a room on the first floor of the house. It was completely devoid of furniture.

"Lovely," the detective said. "Did you fellows do it yourselves or hire a decorator?"

"Mr. Hardy," said the man who carried the gun, "it is my hope that you'll take the questions I'm about to ask you very seriously."

"And if I don't?"

"You'll be here a long time."

"Who are you? Local gangsters? The international mafia? What's this?"

"My name is Stratton," the man replied. "Mr. Rigby here will ask the questions."

"What is it you want?"

"You're investigating the grave of a man by the name of Will Bronson," Rigby said. "Why?"

"Because I've been hired to. That's why."

"What's Bronson to your client?" Stratton questioned.

"My client's interests are confidential."

"Not any more," Rigby said.

"Who is your client?" Mr. Hardy asked.

"That, too, is confidential."

"Hardy, we can find out who hired you!" Stratton threatened.

"Then why did you find it necessary to kidnap me?"

"Kidnap?" Stratton looked surprised. "Are you

under the impression that you've been kidnapped?"

"Mr. Hardy," Rigby added, "nothing could be farther from the truth. You're free to go."

The detective rose. "Thank you."

Stratton placed a large hand on his shoulder. "Just as soon as you tell us who hired you!"

Mr. Hardy refused to answer, and the men refused to release him. Finally, they locked him in the room and left.

While the detective stayed behind as a prisoner, Stratton and Rigby drove to Bayport and pulled up some distance from the Hardy home. They surveyed the house thoroughly.

"How long do we give them?" Rigby asked.

"We wait till the lights go out. Then we go in," Stratton replied.

Ten minutes after the last lamp had been turned off in the house, the men sneaked up to Mr. Hardy's office. Stratton expertly picked the lock and they entered, beaming flashlights around.

"You check the files," Stratton told his companion. "I'll look at this phone log."

For a while, they worked in silence. Suddenly Stratton heard a noise. "Oh-oh," he said. "Light just went on in the house."

"Somebody's coming!" Rigby hissed, and both men looked for a place to hide.

Frank and Joe had heard a muffled sound and had gone downstairs to investigate. Silently they slipped out the back door and approached the office. Joe reached for the door, but Frank pulled him back.

He pointed to the lock. It showed small scratches around the aperture. "Somebody's been inside," Frank whispered. "You wait here."

"You're going in?"

Frank nodded, and Joe decided to go along. Silently Frank opened the door and entered. Joe was right behind him. They scanned the room cautiously.

"Turn on a light," Joe said in a low voice.

"Shh!" Frank warned.

Joe reached for the light switch. It did not work!

"Something's wrong with the lights," the boy said.

Frank, who was halfway across the room, felt a lamp on a table. "I'll tell you what's wrong. Someone's loosened the bulb. I'll just —"

All of a sudden Joe saw something move behind Callie's desk. "Frank, look out!" he cried.

A figure rose in the darkness, pushed Frank and the lamp out of his way, and leaped toward the door.

The second intruder mowed Joe down and the next instant both were gone!

Frank got up and scrambled to his brother's side. "Joe, you all right?"

"I feel like I just went three quarters against the New England Patriots!"

"Stay put. I'll be back." Frank raced outside and saw the two men hurrying toward their car. They climbed in, started the engine, and drove off in a flash.

Instantly Frank jumped on his bike. He took up

the pursuit, not realizing that he was wearing nothing but his underwear!

The two men had a good lead and suddenly made a sharp right turn. By the time Frank reached the intersection, they had disappeared! The road was deserted except for a patrol car that slowly cruised toward the intersection from the left.

Frank paid little attention to it and sped off in the direction the men had taken. He turned to look, however, when a throaty siren blared behind him.

"Excuse me, son!" an officer called out the window. "But we'd like a word with you!"

Crestfallen, Frank stopped his bike. He explained what had happened. The officers, who did not quite believe his story, insisted on escorting him home.

A few minutes later the boy arrived in his father's office with the two policemen in tow. Joe and Aunt Gertrude were waiting anxiously.

"Joe, you want to tell these officers what happened," Frank said, exasperated.

"I'd like to ask the questions, if you don't mind," the taller policeman said. "Ma'am, is Mr. Hardy home?"

"He's due back in the morning," Aunt Gertrude replied.

"Meanwhile, this office was broken into," Frank said. "You can see the pick marks on the door."

The policeman went to look. "Harlan, there are some marks on this lock," he confirmed.

Harlan examined the door, then turned to the

boys. "You fellows have any way of knowing if anything's missing?"

"Just found a lot of open drawers and scattered
papers," Joe replied. "But I lifted a fingerprint off
the filing cabinet."

"Lifting prints takes a specialist," Harlan said.

"I know. I'm a specialist."

"You probably found your own fingerprints, or
your father's."

"No. If you want to go downstairs to our lab, I'll
show you.

"Lab?"

"Sure. It's a perfect match to the print I got off
the cough drops."

"Cough drops???"

"At the cemetery. That means you can use the
license number of that car to get out an APB."

"What car? What APB?" Harlan was thoroughly
confused.

"They didn't turn their lights on tonight. I
couldn't be sure of the plate, but if the prints are
the same, it was probably the same car we saw
following our father in Emmetville, RFB 110."

The officers exchanged glances, still puzzled and
not quite sure of how to handle this matter.

"Look," Harlan said, "we'll put it on the air.
When your father gets back in the morning, ask him
to let us know if anything is missing. I don't even
know if we have a crime for sure. Meantime, you
fellows stay off the streets in your underwear. In
other words, go to bed, all right?"

Frank's eyes lit up. "Bed! That's it!" He turned and ran out of the office.

The officers stared after him in amazement.

"Wish my kid would mind like that," Harlan said wistfully.

"We'll check back in the morning," his colleague promised. "You go to bed too, son. Night, ma'am."

Joe nodded as Aunt Gertrude saw the two policemen out. After they had left, she looked at her nephew in consternation.

"Now, then, what is this all about? Cemeteries, Emmetville? What's this got to do with your father?"

Just then Frank ran down the stairs, carrying a leather-bound notebook. "It's here!" he cried triumphantly.

"What?" Joe asked.

"I don't know exactly, but Dad's notes for the last few days before he left town add up to anything but a vacation. Look!"

Joe stared at the notebook.

"Bronson," Frank went on. "Emmetville Cemetery. That's where we followed him." He turned the page and continued, "Haunt. Hse in Brkdle."

"What?" Joe asked, perplexed.

"It's an abbreviation," Frank said. "I make it out to be Haunted House in Brookdale."

"Now I know we're all having nightmares." Joe chuckled. "Dad's the last man on the face of this earth to believe in haunted houses."

"It's here. His last entry, plus the name Sonny, Tuesday, two A.M."

"That's tomorrow," Joe said.

"No, that's tonight. Two hours past midnight."

Aunt Gertrude instantly knew what the boys had in mind. "Oh, no, you don't!" she said. "Not tonight. Your father will be home in the morning. Now march or you answer to me!"

The boys looked at each other. They knew their aunt meant what she said, yet they had to convince her that they could not stop their investigation now!

"Aunt Gertrude," Frank said evenly, "somebody broke into Dad's office tonight. What if Dad doesn't know what he's up against? What if he's gotten into something over his head? This appointment could be our last chance to warn him!"

"You're starting to sound more and more like your father every day," Aunt Gertrude said. "How would you find that house? Even if you do, it'll be one o'clock before you even get there."

"We'll take the van," Joe said quickly. "When we've located Dad, we can stay at the Trailer Park in Emmetville."

"What if you don't find him?"

"We'll call you on the C.B. either way."

"If you don't, I'll contact the police up there. Then you'll really have something to explain to your father."

"Deal," Frank said. "Come on, Joe, we've got a drive ahead of us!"

The boys dressed quickly, stowed their bikes in the van, and drove off. They discussed the mystery for a while, but finally gave up searching for an answer and continued silently through the night.

They reached the small town of Brookdale around one o'clock in the morning and decided to go to police headquarters to inquire about a haunted house. On the way, they approached a small hill to their right. A Victorian mansion, which had been converted to a night club, was perched on its slope, completely surrounded by trees.

The parking lot in front of the building was filled with cars, and the boys saw couples drifting in and out. The sound of music could be heard in the street.

Just then they noticed a large neon sign over the entrance. It said, THE HAUNTED HOUSE.

Frank drove into the parking lot and stared out

the window in wonder. "I'll be darned!" he exclaimed.

"I feel a whole lot better," Joe said with a grin.

"I'll feel better when we find Dad," Frank declared and parked the van. "I don't see his car."

The boys got out and walked up to the old mansion. The music became louder as they opened the door. They stepped into a room that looked like a funeral parlor. A man in a tuxedo sat at an organ in a corner and played a macabre tune. Frank and Joe walked up to him, feeling uncomfortable.

"We're looking for a — Sonny," Frank said.

"The coffin on your left!" boomed the organ player.

The boys gestured to each other, neither one wanting to go first. Finally Frank went ahead. A few steps led up the side of the coffin.

He looked down. Another set of stairs led into the blackness below. Gingerly Frank started to descend. Suddenly he fell!

"Ohhh!" he cried out.

Joe was close on his heels. "Frank, what is — ohhh!"

The steps ended abruptly and the boys found themselves on a chute, sliding into a dimly lit room below. They were greeted by a chilling laugh. Quickly they got to their feet and stared at a crystal ball with a head inside. It said:

Welcome to the Haunted House. If you survive your ordeal, we look forward to your joining us in the main crypt. If not — happy — hereafter —

Penetrating laughter followed. Frank and Joe walked toward the blank walls of the room, searching for a way out.

"Frank —" Joe whispered.

"Take it easy, Joe. It's just like being in an amusement park." Frank did not sound convincing.

"I'm not having any fun," Joe muttered.

"Here, this way." In the wall, Frank found a panel that moved. He pushed it back and was about to step through, when a skeleton raced out of the opening, nearly knocking the boys over. They jumped aside as it charged into the opposite wall.

"Very amusing," Joe muttered sarcastically, while Frank gestured for his brother to follow him into a mirrored room that had been vacated by the skeleton.

"Now what?" Joe asked.

The boys stared at the many reflecting panels. Some were distortion mirrors, which made them look ten feet tall; others spread their reflections into obesity.

"This way," Frank decided, walking toward a clear panel. But it turned out to be solid glass.

"Here," Joe motioned. "The music seems to be loudest over here." He went toward a mirror that proved to be a short hallway.

Suddenly two doors burst open, admitting the boys into a lively, bizarre room. "Early Frankenstein," Joe thought to himself.

The Haunted House

Cobwebs were draped over tables and chairs. Waiters scurried around with ghoulish white faces, serving drinks to the gaily chatting crowd. The Maitre d' was dressed as Dracula; and Frankenstein, himself, tended bar.

Couples danced to a live band consisting of pipe organ, harpsichord, drums, and bass.

Before the Hardys had a chance to take in further details of their weird surroundings, they were greeted by Dracula. "Have you reservations?" he boomed.

"Ah — would it be possible to talk to Sonny?" Frank inquired.

"Not until he goes on his break."

"We'll just get a couple of cheeseburgers and wait," Frank replied.

Dracula signaled to the Hunchback of Notre Dame, who bounded toward them. "Station twelve," Dracula ordered. The Hunchback grunted and led the boys to an area not far from the band. They sat down, and a girl with white make-up moved up behind them. "Order?" she asked.

"Two cheeseburgers — couple of cokes," Frank replied.

"What do you put on 'em?" Joe wanted to know.

"Everything's on the side," the girl said.

"What're you worrying about cheeseburgers for?" Frank said impatiently. "We've got work to do."

"If we're going to pay for them, they ought to be the way we like them."

The girl turned to leave.

"We're looking for Sonny," Frank told her. "Would you tell him we'd like to talk to him when he gets a break?"

"Sure." She walked off.

"You make some detective," Frank chided his brother. "I'd like to see you try to follow a guy for more than a block without stopping for food."

Joe grinned. "I'm growing. I need nourishment."

"Hey, look. She's telling him about us!" Frank pointed to the band. The waitress was speaking to the wolfman, and both glanced over at the boys. Then the girl went into the kitchen, and the wolfman headed toward the stairs leading to a side exit.

"I think we've found Sonny," Frank murmured.

"He doesn't seem overjoyed to see us," Joe observed. "Let's go!"

They hurried up the stairs Sonny had used and found themselves at the service entrance, which was surrounded by trees and dark shrubbery. They could see no one!

"Sonny!" Frank called out and ran up the hill ahead of him. Joe was right on his heels.

"Sonny?" Frank called again.

"I'll look around the front," Joe said and scooted to the other side of the building. Frank continued up the wooded hill, moving through dark recesses filled with trees and ominous shadows. Suddenly, from out of the darkness, the wolfman lunged at him and sent him flying! Frank was caught by surprise and for a moment felt powerless to escape the desperate fiend who clutched him.

31

They rolled over and over, while Frank tried to find enough leverage to shove Sonny away. "What's the matter with you, pal?" he panted.

Sonny grabbed Frank in a headlock and stared at him through eyes clouded with panic and rage. "What do you want with me? Who are you?" the young man demanded.

"Who are *you?*" Frank countered. "What do you want with my father?"

"Your father?"

Frank's neck was wedged in Sonny's deadly grip, and he found it difficult to talk. "Fenton Hardy," he gasped. "You're supposed to be meeting with him."

Sonny released the pressure. "You're Fenton Hardy's son?"

"Yes, and I'm worried about him."

"How do you know about me?"

"Can I sit up? You're kind of heavy."

Sonny allowed Frank to rise, but hovered over the young detective in anything but a reassuring manner, ready to leap at him at any moment.

"My father's disappeared," Frank explained. "At least I'm afraid he has. I think it has something to do with you."

Sonny stood up and paced back and forth in front of Frank. "How do I know I can trust you?"

"Is he working for you?"

"Yes. But he promised he wouldn't tell anyone. He lied!"

"He always tells my brother and me what he's working on, but he never said anything about you."

"Then how did you find me?"

"Notes in a pad he always keeps. But someone else wanted those notes. They broke into my Dad's office."

Sonny's face paled. He turned to run, but Frank grabbed his arm. "You're not going any place until you tell me about my father! He could be in trouble for helping you. Why did you go to him?"

"I went to your father to find out who I am," Sonny replied.

"Who you are?"

"Somebody's trying to kill me. I don't know why."

Suddenly Joe's voice sounded from the bottom of the hill. "Frank! Frank! Where are you?"

Sonny tensed. "Who's that?"

"My brother. Come on. Let's go someplace where we can talk this out."

Sonny nodded and they walked down the hill. They had almost reached the Haunted House, when Sonny stopped short. He stared at a distinguished-looking man who was getting out of his car near the service entrance.

Frank turned questioningly to his companion. Sonny directed a full swing at him. "You set me up!" he hissed, sending the Hardy boy rolling down the hill. Then he disappeared.

Frank slowly got to his feet, holding his painful chin. Joe ran up to him. "What happened?"

"I found Sonny," Frank replied. "I think somebody is trying to kill him. I've never seen anybody so scared. I'm going after him!"

"I'm coming, too!"

34

"It's almost two o'clock," Frank reminded his brother. "Go inside and see if Dad shows. I'll try and pick up Sonny's trail."

"What if Dad doesn't show?"

"Grab a bike out of the van and come after me!"

Frank ran up the hill into the forest, while Joe returned to the crypt room. At their table, two hamburgers with cheese were waiting for him. He hungrily devoured both.

Two o'clock came and went, but there was no sign of Mr. Hardy. The musicians stopped playing and packed their instruments. People started to walk out, and soon Joe was the only patron left. Busboys began placing chairs on tables, while bright lights illuminated the room, dispelling the bizarre ghostly effect.

The white-faced waitress tapped Joe on the shoulder and asked him to pay their bill. Joe reached into his wallet, but to his great distress, found it empty. Embarrassed, he told the waitress that he had no money.

"What do you mean you can't pay for the two cheeseburgers?" she demanded.

"I can pay for them. I just can't pay for them yet. My brother's got all the bread."

Dracula approached. His theatrical voice had lost its unnatural quality and revealed a Bronx accent. "Hey Madge, they can't close out the register on account of you."

"Talk to this one," the waitress replied. "He says he ain't paying for his two cheeseburgers."

"What was wrong with 'em? You send 'em back?" Dracula asked.

"Send 'em back?" the girl replied. "He ate 'em both. Says his brother's got the money."

"Look," Joe spoke up. "I'll leave you my wallet and my watch. I was expecting my father to meet me here. He's a detective, Fenton Hardy. You can check with the police department. They all know him. I came in here on account of the trouble out back. Keep these, I'll be back to settle up."

Dracula and Madge stared in amazement as Joe thrust his wallet and watch into the girl's hand and hurried out the door.

"Trouble out back?" Madge asked. "What trouble out back?"

Dracula leaned close to the ghoullike waitress. "Keep this under your hat. *We don't want to scare people!*"

Sonny, meanwhile, had hurried deeper and deeper into the woods. He was frightened and confused, and bolted through the undergrowth without watching where he was going. Frank, who had taken up the chase, paused here and there to determine Sonny's trail. In the moonlight he picked up a twig now and then, checking where it had been broken to see which direction his quarry had taken.

Finally Sonny slumped breathlessly against a tree to recover from his uphill climb. Then he made a sharp turn and continued downhill.

Frank was also exhausted and was resting

momentarily when he heard the distant roar of a trailbike. He ran out of the undergrowth and waved wildly. "Joe, Joe! This way!"

Joe heard the indistinct sound of his brother's voice and angled his bike, revving it to a maximum speed as he raced toward the lone figure who stood silhouetted against the trees.

"Dad didn't show," Joe called out.

"That's bad news." Frank panted as he spoke.

"I know. Any sign of Sonny?"

"He reversed himself fifty yards up. Just started to head down the hill."

"Climb on," Joe said.

Frank mounted the trailbike. "Be careful," he warned his brother. "I'm too tired to die."

They sped downhill after Sonny, who had reached the Haunted House and was running toward an old sedan in the parking lot. Suddenly his gaze fell on the man who had frightened him so much before. He was sitting in his car at the far end of the lot, his eyes glued to Sonny's sedan and the Hardy boys' van.

Sonny stopped short in his tracks, but the man had already seen him. Desperately, Sonny charged toward the club's main entrance. The man jumped out of his car and ran after him.

Sonny rushed up to the organ, and for a moment leaned against it breathlessly. It emitted a dissonant cry. Hysterically, Sonny jumped away and looked toward the door. The man had not come in yet.

Sonny scooted up into the coffin and slid down

the chute to the floor below, when the man silently slipped into the funeral room. Seconds later there was a noise in the hallway, and Dracula and two of the waitresses entered through a hidden door. They were tired and eager to get home.

Unaware that a stranger was crouching behind the organ, they walked to the entrance. Dracula stopped at a wall panel and pulled several switches, dousing all the lights in the building. Then the trio went out and locked the door.

Cautiously the stranger stepped out from behind the organ. He looked after the departing employees for a moment, then went to the light box and studied it closely.

Sonny was still sprawled at the foot of the coffin chute in a state of panic. Suddenly a dim light went on and the head of a man appeared, encased in a crystal ball. Terrified, Sonny jumped up and pressed himself against the wall.

"Welcome to the Haunted House," the head said, "the Victorian mansion within whose walls two witches were trapped and burned in sixteen seventy-two."

Sonny ran toward the far wall and crashed into the panel he knew was there. The skeleton burst out and he swiped at it with his right hand, knocking it aside. Then he charged into the hall of mirrors.

The stranger in the funeral room stepped into the coffin and, with a cry of surprise, slid down the chute. The head in the crystal ball appeared before him. "Welcome to the Haunted House —"

The shock of hearing a voice made the man whirl. A chill went down his spine; then he realized the disembodied voice was only a recording. He looked around, trying to find the exit.

Frank and Joe had parked their trailbike and entered the building through the service entrance.

"The place was closing up, Frank," Joe said.

"But his tracks lead to the mansion," his brother replied and opened the door to the darkened discoteque. "See if you can find some matches," he added, "and a candle on one of the tables."

Joe rummaged in his pockets and pulled out a match. He struck it, and the shadows and cobwebs in the room looked frightening in the flickering light.

Frank shivered slightly as he handed Joe a candle in a red glass. Joe lighted it. Carefully they edged forward. Suddenly they heard a rustling noise at the other end of the room. Sonny had entered the disco. He did not know how close his pursuer was.

"Sonny?" Frank called out softly.

"If he didn't want to talk to us before," Joe pointed out, "he isn't going to want to talk to us now."

He was right. Sonny did not reply. Instead, he ducked back into the hall of mirrors.

His shadow entered at the same time, holding a sword he had taken from a shelf on the wall in the other room. When Sonny saw him, he froze in fright.

"I'm going to take you back," the man said in a low voice.

"No!" Sonny cried out.

"I've always been good to you!" the man reminded him and moved forward, trying to figure out which image was the real Sonny.

The young man edged along the wall to the next panel. His mirror images moved as well, confusing his pursuer completely.

"You're not here to help me!" Sonny panted.

"Why do you say that? Do you know who I am?"

Sonny buried his head in his hands. "I know you. You knew me before!"

"Yes, it's all coming back to you, isn't it. That's too bad!" The man still had trouble differentiating the real Sonny from his reflections, but tried not to show it. "If you hadn't run away in Europe, we might have worked it out," he went on. "We can still work it out."

Sonny, however, did not trust him. He lunged across the room in desperate flight. The man went after him with the sword poised. Glass shattered and a mirror fell from the wall. Furiously, the man stabbed another Sonny with his sword, and another, fragmenting panel after panel in a hysterical effort to kill his quarry.

Suddenly he found himself alone in the hall of

mirrors! He rushed to the nearest wall and broke another panel.

Frank and Joe had heard the violent shattering of glass. They realized that Sonny was in danger and tried to make their way to the hall of mirrors. Instead, the only exit they found lead them into an adjoining room, which was decorated as a chamber of horrors. In the eerie candle light, Joe could make out Jack the Ripper, Bluebeard, and other notorious figures of the past.

More glass was broken and the Hardys frantically looked for a way out. Then Sonny slipped into the room. He saw them, stopped short, and threw up his hands in a gesture of despair. "He's here!" he said hoarsely. "He's got a sword!"

"Who?" Joe asked.

Sonny did not reply. "Get out of my way!" he cried.

"Sonny, you have to trust someone," Joe said.

The young man leaped across the room to a panel in the wall and pressed it open. "This way!" he panted.

The boys followed him and the panel snapped shut just before the man with the sword entered the chamber.

Frank, Joe, and Sonny charged out of the service entrance and sprinted to the van. They piled in and drove off with screeching tires, unaware that the man with the sword was watching their departure from the Haunted House!

As they raced through the night, Joe tried to locate his father on the C.B. Instead, Aunt Gertrude answered.

"Where in the world have you been? I've been worried sick!"

"We're fine. We've got Dad's client with us and he's in trouble."

"What kind of trouble?"

Frank gestured to Joe to take it easy.

"Don't worry," Joe said, "Everything is under control. But we're hoping he can help lead us to Dad."

"Your father's fine," Aunt Gertrude said. "He called me half an hour ago."

Frank grabbed the C.B. from Joe. "He called? From where?"

"He was on his way to make sure nothing happened to his evidence."

"What evidence?"

"At the —" Aunt Gertrude realized that she was about to reveal Mr. Hardy's secret. "Never mind. You boys are to get home at once. Your father's orders!"

"Aunt Gertrude, Father doesn't know we have his client with us and that somebody is trying to kill him."

"Oh, dear!" Miss Hardy did not know what to do.

"He could be following us right now," Frank added. "Now where's Dad?"

"He went to the cemetery in Emmetville," Aunt Gertrude said lamely.

"Emmetville. Thanks, Aunt Gertrude. We'll be in touch."

"Now Frank, Frank — " Aunt Gertrude sighed in frustration as the transmission stopped and nothing but static crackled from the set.

Frank turned to Sonny. "You heard her. Our father's out risking his neck for you, just as he promised. Now what's this all about? Why is this man after you?"

Sonny groped to recollect the past. "It keeps coming back in little pieces," he said.

"What's coming back?" Joe asked.

"I was in a military hospital. Navy. They were trying to get me to remember. They said I'd been through a shock of some kind. I didn't seem to want to remember."

"Remember what?" Frank asked.

"Who I am. What happened to me. They told me I worked for our military forces in Europe. That I knew secrets that could help an enemy. I guess I walked off one day and disappeared. When they found me, I didn't even know who I was."

Frank and Joe looked at each other in surprise.

"So, who would want to hurt you?" Frank asked.

"Our country is trying to be friends with the Russians and the Chinese," Sonny replied. "We've been having secret talks with both of them and they told me at the hospital that each side thinks I sold it out to the other. *They* think the Russians and Chinese are all looking for me to find out what I revealed of secret talks."

"*They* think the Russians and Chinese are looking for you?" Joe asked.

"But *you don't*, do you?" Frank put in.

Sonny did not reply. He seemed to become more frightened by the minute. His eyes darted to the back, as if he were afraid someone was following them.

"Someone's looking for you," Joe said.

"Who is he, Sonny?" Frank prodded. "Who is the man with the sword?"

"I don't know," Sonny said lamely, but he did not sound convincing.

"I think you do," Frank said. "You knew who he was when you first saw him from the hill."

Sonny buried his head in his hands.

"It's coming back, Frank. Look at him. He remembers everything!" Joe said.

"If you don't tell us, we can't help you," Frank urged.

Sonny looked up. He seemed to have regained control over himself, and his voice was laced with grim foreboding when he answered, "If I tell you, he'll have to come after *you*, too!"

A chill ran down Frank's spine as he drove along a lonely, deserted road. The countryside was shrouded in mist. They were not aware of another car, with its headlights out, following closely behind. Sonny's enemy was bent over the wheel, looking for an opportunity to strike again!

Frank approached the cemetery in Emmetville and saw his father's car parked in front of the gate. He slowed down.

"Kill the lights," Joe advised.

Frank did.

"There it is," Joe said. "Dad's car."

Frank parked next to it, and the boys climbed out.

"No sign of him," Frank said in a low tone. "We'd better look inside the cemetery."

Joe was apprehensive. "In there?" he asked.

"All right," Frank said. "You stay in the van with Sonny. If I don't come back in five minutes, get out of here. Go for help!"

Joe nodded and the two boys climbed back into the van. Frank waved to them, then disappeared into the darkness. He wondered what had happened to his father since he had seen him in the cemetery earlier that night.

Mr. Hardy was left in the unfurnished room of the one-family house when Stratton and Rigby went to his office. After their return, they talked in muted tones outside, and the detective listened intently to the conversation.

"We've come to the end of the road," he heard Rigby say. Then his former shadow and his companion walked into the room.

"Time to lay our cards on the table, Mr. Hardy," Rigby said.

"You're about to show me your badges," the detective countered, getting up.

Rigby's hand went to his wallet, then he hesitated. "Badges?" he asked.

"CIA, FBI, military investigators. I'd guess Navy first."

The two men looked at each other. Before they could comment, Mr. Hardy went on, "The shoes, the haircut, you have a Navy insignia on your lighter. What did I stumble into?"

"A mess," Stratton replied.

"You're helping a young man," Rigby stated. "I don't know what he's calling himself now, but we want him."

"Why? Who is he?" Mr. Hardy asked.

"He was a Navy attaché working out of NATO. He disappeared for forty-eight hours. The military police found him wandering in his shorts at sub-zero, his recollection of events during those forty-eight hours zero."

"You've gone to a lot of trouble to check out a sailor's binge," Mr. Hardy commented.

"He was military attaché to Commander Buckholtz. He knew every secret in NATO!" Stratton explained.

"Some of our allies think we were sold out," Rigby added.

"And what do *you* think?" Mr. Hardy asked.

"We don't know. When he came back his mind was a complete blank. Something terrible might have happened to him."

"Then why did you turn him loose?"

"We didn't," Stratton replied. "He escaped from a Naval hospital."

"What happens if I tell you where he is?"

"Something has triggered his recall," Rigby said, disregarding Mr. Hardy's question. "He didn't

46

know the name Bronson before. It's possible he can now fill in the forty-eight-hour gap. Tell us what happened."

"I guess I really don't have much choice," Mr. Hardy said. "*If* you're telling me the truth."

"It's the truth," Rigby assured him.

"I'll bring him to you," Mr. Hardy decided. "I won't take you to him."

"Bo —" Stratton began, but was interrupted by a sharp look from his partner.

"I'll give you a number," Rigby said quickly, and wrote it on a piece of paper. "That man belongs in a hospital, Mr. Hardy, where he can get skilled help. Don't try to save him on your own."

Fenton Hardy nodded and walked to the front door. He hesitated, then said, "Are you aware that he thinks someone is trying to kill him?"

Stratton and Rigby exchanged uneasy glances.

"Paranoia isn't unusual in this kind of case," Rigby said.

"Your client is wrong, of course," Stratton added.

Mr. Hardy shrugged and walked out the door.

"You're not really cutting him loose," Stratton asked his partner in surprise.

"Of course not. Stay on him. I'm going to have to do something about that grave," Rigby replied.

"Tonight?"

"When else? By morning the whole thing could have blown up in our faces. Get going and don't lose him!"

Stratton hurried out the door, and Rigby went to

a closet. He pulled out a briefcase, and opened it. A telephone was inside. He pressed several buttons and spoke into the mouthpiece. "This is Rigby. I'm going to need some muscle right now —"

Mr. Hardy left the house and got into his car. As he drove off, he located his sister on the C.B. radio.

"I'm fine," he answered to her worried question. "I told you I'd be away until morning."

"Yes, but Frank and Joe and the police — and those awful burglars —"

"Gert, slow down. What are you talking about? Where are the boys now?"

"Looking for you. They went to Brookdale. A haunted house —"

"Oh, no! Look, when you hear from them, tell them to turn around and get home and wait until I get in touch. This is a very sensitive case and could blow up in my face at any minute."

"Then you get back here right now. Let the police handle it."

"I have a client that requires confidentiality, Gert," Mr. Hardy said. "I promised him that he'd get it. I'm on my way to Emmetville. I've got to protect some evidence. I'll see you in the morning."

"What if the boys don't come back? What if, well — I don't even want to think about it."

"If something serious happens, call the police here in Emmetville. Tell them they can find me at the cemetery."

"The cemetery?"

"Stop worrying. I'm fine. Just don't tell the boys where I am — deal?"

"Deal." Aunt Gertrude signed off. She had been relieved to hear from her brother, but the implications of their conversation made her worry now even more than before.

Mr. Hardy parked his car in front of the Emmetville cemetery and climbed out. He turned up his collar to brace himself against the night's chill, as he slipped through the gate and swiftly walked to the knoll where the Bronson grave had been. It was dark and eerie, and suddenly the detective felt apprehensive as he passed a large monument. Just then a hand reached out from behind it and clutched him around the face. It pulled him to the ground without giving him time to so much as gasp.

Everything went black before Mr. Hardy's eyes, and a few seconds later he was deposited into an empty grave some distance from the monument!

Sonny and Joe had been waiting in the van. Five minutes had passed and Frank had not yet returned. Joe looked impatiently at his watch. "I wonder what he's doing in there so long," he muttered.

Neither was aware that Sonny's pursuer had parked his car behind them and was watching the van intently.

Joe could not wait any longer. "I'm going in there," he declared.

"He said to wait," Sonny objected.

"I'm leaving you the keys," Joe assured him. "Take off if we don't come back." With that, he climbed out of the van and ran into the cemetery. Without hesitation, he walked toward the knoll where he had seen his father looking at a grave. He could make out his brother's dark silhouette, as Frank scanned one tombstone after another.

"Frank!" Joe called out softly.

"I told you to stay in the van!" Frank seemed annoyed.

"I got worried about you. Where's Dad?"

"I can't find him. Figured he'd be someplace near the grave he was looking at earlier. My guess is it says Bronson on it, but I can't find it."

"I'll help you look," Joe offered.

"No. Somebody's got to stay with Sonny. He might take off, and he's our only link with Dad."

"I'll go back and get him."

"Okay. I'll keep looking for the grave."

Joe disappeared into the darkness and Frank resumed his search for the Bronson burial site. Suddenly, with a gasp of surprise, he fell into a black, gaping hole!

"Help!" he cried out, feeling a sharp pain shooting through his right leg. "Joe! Joe!"

But Joe was already too far away to hear him.

In the meantime, Sonny had become increasingly apprehensive about the two boys. He looked at his watch and finally decided to go after them. He jumped out of the van and turned toward the cemetery, when his shadow appeared from behind a tree and stepped up to him.

"Hello, Will."

Sonny stood stock still. Fear and panic showed in his face, then gave way to sudden resignation. Unable to move, he made no attempt to flee.

"Hello, Commander," he replied, with little emotion left in his voice.

"Commander?" the man repeated. "It was always Jack. You don't know how it pains me to be here now, like this. You were a son to me."

"I felt the same way. You were the father I never had. I couldn't believe you'd done it. I wouldn't believe it. I guess that's why I blacked out."

"You shouldn't put anyone too high on a pedestal," the commander said. "Will, we're all human. If you'd given me a chance to explain —"

"How could you explain selling us out?"

"I was being blackmailed for something I did, Will. Something human. But it would have cost me everything. My career, my family — I didn't think the papers I sold them were really that important."

"It wasn't your decision to make!" Sonny declared.

"I'm not a bad man, Will. You know that. You were my aide for two years."

"If you're not a bad man," Sonny said, "what are you going to do now?"

"You're going to have to come with me."

"Because you don't have any choice —"

"That's right, Will. I don't have any choice." The

man walked closer to Sonny and grabbed him with his left hand. His right was in his pocket, pointing a gun at Sonny!

Back in the cemetery, Frank lay in the black hole and moaned with pain. Suddenly he heard someone else groan. He pulled his flashlight from his pocket and shone it around, realizing he had fallen into an empty grave. On the ground next to him lay his father!

"Dad!"

"Thank goodness," Fenton Hardy said, slowly coming to. "Are you all right?"

"I can't stand on my ankle, but I'll be fine. Who did this to you?"

"Some intelligence guys from the Navy. They had no intention of hurting me but they didn't want me to see what they were doing, either."

"What were they doing?"

"As near as I can figure it, they were robbing an empty grave."

"Huh?" Frank was dumfounded.

"They faked the death of Will Bronson. I guess you know him as Sonny. He did something that was quite an embarrassment to our friends in the military."

"Sold some secrets. I know about that, but he didn't do it. He told us —"

"He told you?" Fenton Hardy jumped up. "You mean his memory has come back?"

"Yes, and someone's after him."

"He could be in real danger, Frank. Where's Joe?"

"Making sure Sonny doesn't run off," Frank replied and quickly told his father what had happened.

Mr. Hardy had an uneasy feeling about the situation and decided to go and see if the two were still in the van. He told Frank to stay where he was until they picked him up, then he climbed out of the grave and ran toward the gate.

Commander Buckholtz pushed Sonny into his car and made him sit behind the wheel. "You drive!" he ordered.

Sonny started the engine. "Hurry. Get out of here!" his tormentor urged. "Someone's coming!"

He had noticed Joe sprinting toward the van. Seconds later Mr. Hardy ran through the gate. When he heard Joe starting the engine, he gesticulated wildly, trying to stop him. "Joe!"

"Out of my way, Dad!" Joe yelled, putting the vehicle into reverse gear.

"What are you doing?" Mr. Hardy shouted as Joe moved backwards. "Have you lost your —"

The commander pointed his gun at Sonny. "Let's go!" Then he noticed the van coming toward them and screamed. "Look out!"

With a sickening crunch, Joe backed into the front end of the commander's car. The man was momentarily thrown forward, and Sonny lunged across to get the gun. When he reached into the man's pocket, he realized that there was no weapon. His tormentor had merely pretended to have a pistol!

Joe jumped from the van and charged toward the car. Fenton Hardy rushed up at the same instant. But the commander had enough time to leap out and run into the cemetery. Joe and Mr. Hardy followed in hot pursuit.

"Stop him, Dad!" Joe called to his father, and both chased the fugitive into the dark shadows of the graveyard. He ran to the knoll, then changed his direction and angled off to the right. Suddenly he dropped out of sight!

"Ahhh!" he cried out when he fell into the empty grave and landed next to Frank.

The moon had partially emerged from behind a cloud, casting an eerie light in the grave.

The boy blinked in utter astonishment. "Hello!" he said.

Commander Buckholtz turned to stare at Frank and mumbled an incoherent reply. He looked as if he had seen the last ghost his constitution could handle, and promptly passed out. Seconds later Joe, Fenton Hardy, and Sonny reached the grave. After cries of surprise and explanations all around, Joe went to call the police and an ambulance for Frank. The commander was taken into custody, and Frank's ankle was examined at the nearest hospital. Luckily it was only a sprain, and he was released the same night.

The following morning Rigby and Stratton arrived at the Hardy house for a conference. Sonny, who had spent the night at the detective's home, was present, and so was Callie, who could hardly wait to hear what had happened.

Mr. Hardy paced back and forth in his office. "The Navy thought you had sold them out because some files were missing," he said to Sonny. "In order to throw the other side off, they claimed that you had died. That prevented a trial and public embarrassment."

"That's why you had a phony grave," Joe added.

"We were very thorough," Stratton admitted. "Unfortunately, we knew Mr. Hardy would order the grave dug up. They'd find it empty and our whole story about your death would be exposed."

"So we got the empty coffin out of there," Rigby said. "We were just trying to protect you, Bronson. We were sure you hadn't taken the files but we didn't know who had, and you couldn't help us."

"When Will Bronson escaped," Frank said, "he made himself a sitting duck for the one who really stole the papers."

"Listen," Stratton said, "I'll admit some of us weren't so sure he hadn't escaped because he was guilty. I've never put much stock in that amnesia business."

"I didn't want to believe what the commander did. I guess I just cracked —" Sonny's voice trailed off.

"What'll happen to the commander?" Callie asked.

"What happens to anyone who breaks the rules.

He's going to have to pay," Stratton said.

"Court martial," Rigby added. "The end of a career. Probably imprisonment."

"A sad finish to a great career," Sonny mused.

"The boys and I have talked a lot about not letting down at the end," Mr. Hardy spoke up. "How

many great games are thrown away in the fourth quarter?"

"If you ask me," Joe said, "Will came through pretty good in the fourth quarter."

"That's right," Rigby admitted. "Will, I think the Navy'll be pleased with your report and I want to

thank you, Mr. Hardy, and your two boys."

"Let us know next time Navy Intelligence needs help with a case," Mr. Hardy smiled. "I'll see if the boys are available."

Rigby and Stratton laughed, and Callie threw her arms around Frank. He turned red.

Joe rolled his eyes. "If only I were two years older!" he said longingly.

Just then Aunt Gertrude entered and hugged the younger boy. Joe made a face.

Flight to Nowhere

*T*he huge stadium was packed with young people as a rock concert neared its end. Psychedelic lights undulated over the stage, and Tony Bird, the teenage idol, belted out one of his most popular songs, accompanied by his band, *The Flickering Torch*.

Tony finished his number to tumultuous applause. People rose to their feet and shouted for more. However, the performers waved good-by and resolutely clambered offstage.

Wiping beads of perspiration from his forehead, Tony Bird, a good-looking young man in his twenties, moved through the wings. He was searching for the detective he was to meet to discuss crowd control at his next concert in Bayport. Finally his eyes focused on a tall, distinguished-looking man with gray hair who pushed his way toward him.

They exchanged smiles, unable to get close enough to say hello. As they weaved through the shoving crowd, young girls with moist eyes fought for a touch or even a glimpse of their favorite rock star, while the more sophisticated ones begged for autographs. Tony smiled, scribbled his name here and there, and finally managed to escape from his fans to a secluded part of the backstage area. Fenton Hardy, the detective, arrived seconds later, looking as if he had been through a wringer.

Tony laughed. "Welcome to the world of rock concerts, Mr. Hardy. It's even more fun trying to get *out* of the stadium. Want to change your mind?"

The detective grinned. "I have to admit running that gauntlet was a little daunting. I haven't had much experience with this kind of crowd control. But by the time you play Tricities Stadium, I'll have acquired some expert help."

"Oh?"

"I have two sons, who, judging by the size of their record collection, should know all there is to know about it. And about you. They've got every album you've ever recorded. They're going to be thrilled to meet you."

"Didn't you tell me they sometimes help you in your work?" Tony asked.

"Yes, they do," Fenton Hardy replied.

"They sound like quite a team."

"Well, despite their skills, they're ordinary, everyday boys," Mr. Hardy said with a modest smile.

While their father had gone to New York to meet with Tony Bird, Frank and Joe Hardy had set off in a single-engine Piper Comanche on a different assignment. They were floating through the blue sky above a dense cloud cover.

Joe, who was taking lessons from his brother, sat at the controls. With a whoop of joy he guided the small craft into a roll. Frank, who was not happy about the unexpected maneuver, struggled in his seat as the plane continued to glide on its back.

"How's that, teach?" Joe asked, exhilarated.

"Terrific. Now put it back," Frank replied.

"How do you do that?"

The boy sighed in comic exasperation. "Dad gets to go to New York and work with Tony Bird, and I get to work with you. How did that happen?"

Joe smiled. "Just lucky, I guess."

Frank leaned over to the controls. "Do you mind if I help myself?" Expertly he righted the small plane.

Then he turned to his brother. "Number one rule of aviation. Before you can fly upside down, you have to learn how to fly right-side up."

"Sounds logical," Joe agreed, resuming control of the plane. Then he brought up the subject of work again.

"Frank, this new case we're on *is* interesting."

"It is?"

"A normal, everyday guy has a good job and a brand-new wife. One morning he leaves the house after breakfast. 'Good-by honey, see you tonight. I won't be late,' and disappears into thin air. Why?"

"She burned the toast?" Frank kidded.

Joe grimaced. "Which would you rather be handling, an intriguing missing person's case, or crowd control for Tony Bird?"

Frank's silence was eloquent.

"Okay," Joe said sheepishly. "Don't answer that."

Flight to Nowhere

Just then a voice cut in over the radio. "This is Eastwick Field. Advisory — all planes in the area — we have a pilot alert —"

The Hardy boys looked at each other in concern as the warning continued.

"Skyhawk, one-niner-whiskey, instrument malfunction. At last radio contact, he was proceeding at four thousand feet, course one-three-o, over Wheeling Power Station. All planes in the area, exercise extreme caution!"

Frank said tensely. "Four thousand over Wheeling Power. That's too close for comfort. Take her up to five thousand, Joe."

Joe hauled back on the stick. "He'll never get through that soup without instruments."

Frank took the microphone and held it close to his mouth. "Eastwick, this is Comanche eight-three-foxtrot. We are leveling at five thousand feet in area of lame duck. Can he divert? Over."

"We have you, eight-three-foxtrot," was the reply. "Negative. All fields within range are ILS. Ceiling three hundred feet or below. Over."

Joe lowered the Comanche into the clouds. Almost at once the disabled Skyhawk appeared in front of them, flying straight at the Hardy Boys!

Frank reached over, grabbed the controls from his brother, and banked the plane sharply to port. They barely missed hitting the Skyhawk.

Joe held his breath as Frank expertly brought their craft around again. "Take over," he said tersely. "This is no time for practice."

64

Frank nodded and spoke into the microphone. "Eight-three-foxtrot, Eastwick. We have visual contact. Prepare emergency equipment. We'll try to lead him down. Over."

"We copy, eight-three-foxtrot," was the reply. "Good luck."

"Better make sure he knows we want him to follow us and not hit us," Joe said.

As the Comanche circled and approached the other plane again, Frank gestured to the Skyhawk's pilot, indicating that he was to fly behind them. The man, who was still upset about the near miss, nodded grimly.

Frank eased the stick forward. "Here we go."

"I hope he's good," Joe said.

"You hope *he's* good!"

Joe chuckled as both planes disappeared into the clouds. At times the Skyhawk's nose was right on the Comanche's tail, and Frank as well as the other pilot hunched tensely over the controls. The air traffic controller in the small tower followed the descent closely through a pair of binoculars, while an emergency truck rolled up to the runway.

Finally the narrow field with a single hangar and a small office building came into view. Frank guided the Comanche onto the only strip and landed safely, taxiing down the runway and swinging off to one side.

Joe turned and noticed that the Skyhawk was right behind them. "He's down!" the boy exulted. "He made it!"

Frank sat back and stretched his aching neck muscles. "Well, now that we're here, let's find the man we came to see."

He opened the cockpit door and the boys jumped out of the small plane. They walked across the runway and approached a young man in overalls.

"Where can we find Lou Haskell?" Frank inquired.

"You just brought him down. Lucky for him you boys were up there," the youth replied.

Frank and Joe nodded their thanks and went to the Skyhawk. The pilot was emerging from his cockpit.

"Mr. Haskell?" Frank asked.

"Just what did you two think you were doing up there?" the man thundered. "You know how close we came to a head-on collision?"

Joe's temper flared. "If we hadn't been up there, you wouldn't be down here!"

Frank put a restraining hand on his brother's arm, and looked straight at the pilot. "We were trying to help you."

"I was perfectly capable of getting down," Haskell replied with clipped speech.

"That's not what you told the tower," Frank reminded him.

Haskell walked toward the hangar and the boys followed. "The tower was panicking for no good reason," he grumbled. "You boys shouldn't be up in a plane if you don't know how to handle it."

"I know how to handle a plane," Frank said evenly. "That's why you're still alive, Mr. Haskell!"

Haskell glanced at him. "How do you know my name?"

"We came here to see you."

"What about?"

"We understand that Richard Johnston did some work for your company, All Points Airways," Joe explained.

Haskell paused just before entering the hangar. The boys noticed a chain-link-enclosed dog run next to it. Two large Dobermans were inside.

"That's right," Haskell replied. "You friends of Dick's?"

"No, sir," Frank said. "Our father was hired by his wife to find him. He's disappeared."

Haskell looked from one boy to the other. When he spoke again, his voice had lost much of its edge. "Come in," he invited.

They entered the dim hangar and walked toward a gleaming small passenger jet. On its side were the words *All Points Airways*. Frank noticed it briefly but his attention was focused on Haskell, whose mood seemed to have changed completely.

"I'm sorry I took your heads off like that just now," the man said. "I guess I was more scared by what happened up there than I wanted to admit. I wouldn't have made it down to the field without you." He shook his head and smiled ruefully. Then he put his arms around both boys.

"Must be getting defensive in my old age. Thank you." Haskell let them go and paused under the left wing of the beautiful little jet. "You say Dick has disappeared?"

"He left the house yesterday morning and hasn't been heard from since," Frank replied.

"I know his wife. She might be overreacting. He could have been called out of town —"

Joe shook his head. "Not without telling her. He took no clothes, no briefcase, no equipment."

"Did she file a missing-person's report with the police?" Haskell asked.

"Yes. But — they've got a backload that reads like a telephone directory."

"When was the last time you saw him?" Frank asked Haskell.

"It's been two weeks, at least."

"I understood he had an appointment with you yesterday."

"He never showed up. Is that when he disappeared?"

"Yes," Frank replied. "What about friends, someone he might have gone to in a moment of trouble, distress, someone here at the field, or —"

"I wish I could help you boys," Haskell interrupted. "But I never really knew Richard very well."

"Johnston was an audio engineer," Joe said. "Could you tell us what he did for All Points Airways?"

"Sure." Haskell put a hand on the plane's wing. "He designed the sound system for this baby."

The boys moved closer to the Gulfstream jet. "That's some bird," Joe said admiringly. "I've never been on one of these."

"Could we —" Frank began, but Haskell cut him off.

"I'm afraid not. I just got it spic and span for a client. Another time." He glanced at his watch. "That little incident in the sky has me running about half-an-hour late. I don't think there's any thing more I can tell you about Dick."

The boys realized Haskell wanted them to leave, and Frank took the hint. "Thanks for your help, Mr. Haskell."

"We appreciate it," Joe added.

Haskell ushered them toward the hangar door. "I appreciate your help up there. I owe you a debt that's not going to be easy to pay off." He shook hands with them. "Thanks again," he added.

The boys left without looking back. Haskell stood in front of the hangar for a moment, expressionless, then turned his attention to the Dobermans, who had begun to bark loudly and ferociously, clawing at the wire barricade to get out.

When Frank and Joe arrived home, they parked their van in front of their well-tended two-story house. They jumped out and went inside. The door to their father's office was open, and they noticed their Aunt Gertrude standing in the reception area, speaking into the telephone. A brightly colored casette tape lay on the desk beside her.

"I'll let you know the moment I hear from them," Miss Hardy was saying. When she saw the boys, she put a hand over the receiver. "It's Leslie Johnston," she whispered.

Frank took the telephone, while Joe picked up the tape. It was Tony Bird's latest recording.

"Mrs. Johnston, this is Frank Hardy."

"Hello Frank. Did you find Lou Haskell at the airport?"

"Yes, we did see Mr. Haskell and he did have an appointment with your husband yesterday. But your husband didn't arrive."

There was a slight pause. "What do we do now?" Leslie Johnston asked.

"We've still got a couple of other names to check out," Frank said. "We're doing all we can, Mrs. Johnston."

"I know that. But it's been almost two days, and I'm really worried."

"I'm sure we're going to find him," Frank assured her lamely, "and everything's going to be all right. We'll let you know as soon as we have any news." He hung up.

"She's taking it pretty badly, right?" Joe said.

"She's frightened," Frank replied. "She's watching her whole life start to break apart around her because the most important person in it is suddenly gone. She doesn't believe she'll ever see him again."

"Is he the kind of man who would just walk out on a situation he didn't like?" Aunt Gertrude asked.

"That's what we're trying to find out," Joe told her.

They heard voices from Mr. Hardy's inner office, and Joe asked, "Is Dad home?"

"He has some company," Aunt Gertrude replied with a slight smile.

Just then Fenton Hardy emerged from his office with a group of men. One of them was Police Chief Collig, an old friend of the Hardy family. Another was Tony Bird, whom the boys recognized from the many photographs they had seen of him. The third was a modishly dressed, elegant man of about forty.

"We'll go over the layout of the stadium and see how many extra men we need," Mr. Hardy was saying. Then he noticed the boys and smiled. "Tony, Mr. Fry, I'd like you to meet my sons Frank and Joe."

Everyone shook hands, and Mr. Hardy explained that Carl Fry was Tony Bird's manager. Frank smiled at the rock star. "We're tremendous fans of yours, Mr. Bird."

"Let's make that Tony, and I need all the fans I can get."

Joe still held the cassette. "Is this the new one?" he asked the singer.

"Hot off the presses," Tony confirmed. "Hasn't even been released yet."

Mr. Hardy addressed his sons. "I'm going down to the stadium now. I'll be back after lunch. Any luck with the Johnston disappearance?"

"Nothing, Dad," Joe replied.

"We've checked every hospital, morgue, and police department within fifty miles," Frank added.

Chief Collig shrugged. "I'd say the man just turned mother's picture to the wall, drove to an airport, and took a plane to somewhere he's never been. Happens every day."

Frank shook his head. "Not to a couple like the Johnstons," he insisted.

"You're not talking about Richard Johnston, are you?" Tony inquired.

They all looked at him in surprise. "Yes. Do you know him?" Fenton Hardy asked.

"I gave him his start. He's the best sound technician in the country. I'll only use his stuff. I've gotten him contracts all over the world. Figured he'd be wiring up the amps at the stadium. What's happened to him?"

"We don't know," Fenton Hardy said. "He hasn't been seen since yesterday morning."

Carl Fry glanced restlessly at his watch. "If we're going to review the security arrangements at the stadium, might I suggest we get going? I do have an appointment with the television people at four." His voice had an acid edge to it.

"Yes, of course," the detective said. Then he turned to the boys. "Keep digging. We'll meet on it later in the day."

Frank and Joe watched the men walk out the door.

"Maybe Callie will turn something up," Frank said hopefully.

Callie was Mr. Hardy's part-time secretary and a good friend of the boys'. Presently she was on an errand in connection with their investigation.

The boys went into the living room and Frank sat down next to their C.B. equipment. Joe paced back and forth restlessly.

"Wearing a groove in the carpet is not going to get us any nearer to finding Richard Johnston," Frank said philosophically.

"I've got to be doing something when I can't be doing anything," Joe mumbled.

Frank tried to make sense of his brother's statement. "I may have to work that out," he said.

"Did you notice how Haskell's attitude changed toward us once we mentioned Johnston?" Joe asked. "From Mr. Hyde the guy was back to Dr. Jeckyl, arms around our shoulders."

"Almost losing his life has a way of making a person irritable," Frank suggested.

"Tell me about it."

"I'd like you to tell *me* about it," Tony Bird said as he walked through the door.

"I thought you'd gone to the stadium." Frank sounded surprised.

"I leave those kinds of arrangements to your father and my manager. I'm still getting over the shock of Richard Johnston's disappearance. Tell me what you know about it."

"Zero," Joe replied promptly. "That's our problem."

The C.B. radio crackled and Callie's voice was heard. "Breaker, breaker, this is Calico calling *Los Hermanos*. Come in breaker. Breaker —"

Frank picked up the microphone. "Calico, this is *Los Hermanos*. Where are you?"

"On a turn-out five miles outside of Eastwick on Route Twenty-seven. I think I've got something."

"We read you, Calico. What have you got?"

"I'd rather show you."

"We're on our way. That's a ten-four." Frank put down the mike.

"I'd like to come with you," Tony spoke up. "Dick's a very old friend."

"We've only got a van. It's not exactly a limousine." Joe grinned.

"Are you kidding? I've traveled around this country, doing one night stands for twelve years in a van that was held together by some rusty nails and pieces of string. Let's go."

Flight to Nowhere

Tony and the Hardy boys drove to the spot Callie
had designated. It was a deserted area with a steep
cliff on one side. Frank parked next to Callie's car
and they got out.

The girl was standing at the edge of the precipice
and peered down. "Over here!" she called out.

When they joined her, they noticed the guard rail
had been broken and a car had crashed down the
cliff. Callie did not know whose it was or whether
anyone had been in it. By the time she had arrived
at the spot, the accident had already occurred.

Quickly the boys tied a rope to the bumper of the
van and Joe climbed to the bottom of the precipice
to investigate.

"Can you see the license number?" Tony asked the group at the top.

"No, but the year and the make are right," Frank said grimly.

Joe moved toward the wreck and shouted, "Houdini couldn't have gotten out of this!"

Callie's eyes filled with tears. "Mrs. Johnston is such a nice person. How are we going to break this to her?"

Joe reached the wreck and peered through the windows. Those that were not shattered were shut, the smashed frames had been squeezed together, and the doors had buckled. Joe whistled. "The car's empty!" he called.

He went back to the rope and began to climb up. Meanwhile, the trio at the top stared thoughtfully at the wreck.

"How did you find it, Callie?" Frank asked.

"Mrs. Johnston said that when her husband left yesterday morning, he was low on gas. I checked at the station he usually goes to. It's at the turnoff to Route Twenty-seven. The attendant remembered him because he was in a hurry to get to Eastwick Field."

"Eastwick Field?" Tony echoed.

"That's right," Frank said.

Joe's head appeared over the cliff and he pulled himself to the roadside. He was out of breath and looked puzzled. "That wreck down there — no human being could have crawled out of it."

"Are you sure of that?" Frank asked.

76

"Not unless he was a midget and as thin as a pencil."

"Which means nobody was *in* the car when it went over."

Joe nodded. "And take a look at this, Frank. I noticed it coming in —" he pointed to the ground.

Since twilight had fallen, Frank took a small six-cell flashlight from his pocket and beamed it on the area. There were tire tracks leading to the edge of the asphalt from the opposite direction!

"Those are leading *from* Eastwick Field, not *to* it!" Joe exclaimed.

"But Haskell told us Johnston never got there," Frank said.

"Lou Haskell?" Tony asked in surprise.

"You know him?"

"Sure," Tony replied. "I keep my Gulfstream at Eastwick."

"Then that jet we saw there is yours!" Joe declared.

"I lease it from Haskell," Tony explained.

"He was very reluctant to let us go inside," Frank stated.

"You can take a look 'round it any time you want to," Tony told them. "But what has that got to do with Dick's disappearance?"

Frank looked thoughtful. "It might help us find out."

"No problem," Tony said.

"Mr. Haskell wasn't very enthusiastic about his come-back-anytime invitation," Joe pointed out.

Tony shrugged. "It's my plane. I'm telling you, there's no big deal. We'll go there right now."

Even though it was almost dark, the Hardys took him up on the invitation. Callie begged off, saying she had to go home. She said good-by to everyone, then the young people parted and went in opposite directions.

When Tony and the Hardys arrived at the airport, the hangar looked ghostly in the moonlight. The large doors were closed, and the dog run was empty.

The boys parked the van a short distance away, climbed out, and walked toward the building with Tony.

"It looks locked up," Joe said.

Tony reached into his pocket. "I have a key. I told you, I don't know what you expect to accomplish here, but there's no problem getting in." He unlocked the hangar doors and pushed one open. "There you are."

The three went into the building. It was dark, with only a sliver of moonlight falling through the open door.

"Gotta be a light somewhere here," Tony said, fumbling for a switch near the entrance.

"I've still got my flashlight," Frank said and clicked it on. Suddenly a low rumbling noise came from the door.

"Frank!" Joe cried in alarm.

Frank whirled, shining the beam behind them. The two Dobermans, their teeth bared, stood between the three young people and the door, growling ferociously!

Frank, Joe, and Tony froze in terror. Frank kept his light trained on the dogs, who snarled without moving forward.

Tony nervously cleared his throat. "Lou never had to employ guard dogs to protect my plane before," he muttered.

"I wonder when they were last fed," Frank added softly.

"From the looks of them, I'd say sometime in nineteen forty-eight," Joe quipped weakly.

"There's an office at the back —" Tony suggested.

"We'd never make it," Frank decided. "Back up — slowly —"

Still facing the dogs, the trio retreated in the direction of the Gulfstream. The dogs, with the light shining in their eyes, hesitated for a moment but finally barked ferociously and lunged forward. The loud noise set off an alarm, and from the corner of his eye Frank saw a red light go on on one wall of the hangar.

"Here they come!" he cried out. "Run!"

"Just what I had in mind," Joe panted.

Tony and the Hardys made a dash for the Gulfstream while the dogs rapidly narrowed the gap between them. The young people reached the rear gangway and dashed up the stairs. In a flash, they disappeared through the hatch. Joe closed it behind them with a sigh of relief.

Flight to Nowhere

The dogs stopped at the bottom and continued to bark viciously, while the trio stood panting in the airplane.

"Comforting to know I'm so well guarded," Tony muttered.

"Oh, absolutely," Joe added sarcastically. "But now what?"

"I was hoping you had an idea," Frank said.

"I was hoping the same thing," Joe told him.

"Why me?"

"You're older."

"Thanks."

"We could throw them some meat and while they're eating, make a run for it," Joe suggested.

"Sounds good," Frank said.

"Only one problem," Joe corrected himself.

"What's that?" Tony asked.

"We're the only meat we've got."

"That *is* a problem," Tony admitted.

While the dogs prowled restlessly around the Gulfstream, Frank illuminated its plush interior with his flashlight. "This is some setup," he said admiringly.

"It's cozy," Tony said. "I like to travel in style. That's usually because I don't like the place I'm headed for."

Frank noticed a tool kit protruding from under a seat. He kneeled down and dragged it out. A strip with lettering across its top read, *Johnston's Sound Systems*. "Hey, look at this!" he exclaimed.

Tony and Joe moved closer.

"This proves that Johnston was here!" Frank went on.

"Not necessarily," Joe objected. "He could have left it behind a couple of weeks ago."

Just then Frank's flashlight beam fell on Tony Bird's new album on cassette. "That's possible," he said, "except for this!" He pointed to the cassette.

Tony picked it up. "How did this get here? It hasn't been released yet. In fact, only half a dozen of them were made a few days ago."

Frank whistled. "Who has those cassettes, Tony?"

"I've got two of them, and the record companies in New York and L.A. have two, and I gave one to your father — and I sent one to Richard Johnston. I wanted his opinion on the sound quality. We had a few technical bugs I wanted worked out."

"Then Johnston was here, which means Haskell lied to us!"

Tony stared in disbelief. "Why would he do that?"

"I don't know — yet."

Tony shook his head. "I took this baby out last week. I could have left this tape in here."

Joe pulled a handkerchief out of his pocket and wrapped it around his right hand. Then he carefully took the cassette from Tony. "We'll check for prints," he said.

Before anyone could comment, bright lights illuminated the Gulfstream and Collig's voice boomed through the hangar. "This is the police! Come out of that airplane!"

Frank sighed. "We'd be delighted."

"We can't tell them anything that would alarm Haskell," Joe warned.

"We won't," Frank assured him.

Tony led the way out of the jet. It was surrounded by police; the hangar doors were wide open; and headlights bathed the interior with light. He noticed that both dogs had been muzzled by airport security guards.

"Good to see you, Sheriff," Tony said brightly. "Just showing my friends, the Hardy boys, my plane. The dogs must have set off the alarm."

"I know that's why *you* think they're here, Mr. Bird," the chief said. "Question is, is that why *they* think they're here."

Frank and Joe exchanged looks as Collig continued, "This wouldn't have anything to do with that car that went over the cliff? The one Callie reported to me, or the tire tracks that lead in this direction?"

Frank smiled. "Sheriff, you know how you're always telling us not to come to you without hard facts."

"Yeah."

"We don't have any," Joe confessed.

The boys and Tony walked past Chief Collig and the dogs. Frank turned. "Thanks for your help, Sheriff." He patted one of the muzzled Dobermans. "Nice doggie."

The chief looked exasperated. "Why is it even when they do what I say, I figure they're putting one over on me?"

Frank, Joe, and Tony did not reply. With a grin, they left the hangar.

Later that night the two boys were busy in the basement of their home. Joe showed Frank three glass slides with powdered fingerprints on them and said, "This will tell us." He put the first one under a microscope. "This is from the silver cigarette case Mrs. Johnston sent over. No one's touched it since her husband left."

Frank looked into the microscope and studied the whorls. Then Joe changed slides. The next one was a different print.

"I'd say that belonged to Tony Bird," Joe declared, looking over his brother's shoulder. "But

look at this!" He slipped in the third slide, which was identical to the first.

"I took that off the cassette also," he explained. "That proves that Richard Johnston was at that airport and in the plane!"

"Which means that Haskell was lying," Frank declared, "and that Johnston may have more of a link to Tony Bird than he's led us to believe."

"You don't think Haskell could have anything to do with Johnston's disappearance?"

"I'm just considering all the possibilities, Joe."

"One thing's for sure."

"What's that?"

"We're going to be at that concert tomorrow!"

The next day, technicians were setting up for the evening's performance at Tricities Stadium. The speakers were delivered just as Frank and Joe arrived. They walked toward their father, who stood in front of several young men and women, displaying a large seating chart and explaining their duties to them.

"The main thing," Mr. Hardy said, "is to know the difference between somebody who's just having a good time and someone who might cause trouble. Now if you think somebody might be a problem, alert me or one of the uniformed officers before you do anything."

"Excuse me, Dad," Frank interrupted. "Is Tony Bird here yet?"

"In his dressing room," the detective replied.

"Tell the guard I said it's all right." He turned back to his group and continued, "As to dress, you'll all wear street clothes as if you were members of the audience, but you'll each have one of these." The detective held up a clip-on security badge for the young people to see.

Meanwhile, Frank and Joe went to the dressing-room area. They approached a uniformed guard and pointed to Mr. Hardy. The guard nodded and let them pass. They stopped outside Tony Bird's room, and were about to enter when they heard the agitated voices of the singer and his agent through the door.

"I told you I wanted it today!" Tony said.

"What's the rush?" Carl Fry asked defensively. "You've got a concert tonight."

"There's no rush. But I've been asking you for months, and you've always got some excuse."

"I don't understand this, Tony. I really don't. I've been handling your finances — your dates — for what — five years now? And you've done pretty good. This sounds like you don't trust me."

"I didn't say that, Carl," Tony said evenly. "I just want to know how much money I've got and where it is."

"You're a very rich guy. The money's in stocks, bonds, real estate —"

"Don't forget about insurance," Tony put in. "I've got more coverage than the Trade Center."

"Look," Fry went on, "when you hired me, you said, 'I'm a singer. I don't want to worry about

86

business. You sign the checks. You pay the bills. You make the investments.' You didn't want to be bothered."

"Well, I want to be bothered now. I want it spelled out in black and white. And I want it before I take off for London in the morning."

"You've got it," Fry said. "No problem."

"There's one more thing —"

"What's that?"

"Richard Johnston. He should be here wiring up this equipment, but he's been missing for days. He didn't get in touch with you, did he, Carl?"

"Not for a couple of weeks."

"How was he the last time you talked to him?"

"Fine. Told me he'd see me here at the concert."

Tony nodded.

"If there's nothing else, I've got some problems with the publishing of *Pretty Girls* I've got to work out," Fry said, and turned to leave.

"Carl," Tony said, "let me have a copy of our contract, too."

Fry hurried out of the room and almost collided with Frank and Joe, who were coming in.

"We've got some news," Frank told Tony.

The rock star picked up his guitar. "Tell me on the way to the stage. I'm already late for rehearsal."

As they walked out, Joe said in a low voice, "We've matched a fingerprint of Johnston's to one of those on the cassette. That puts him in your plane within the last few days."

"I'll talk to Haskell tonight before the concert,"

Tony decided. "You boys are right. There's something going on, and somehow I'm involved. You've got to find that connection."

There was scattered applause from the assembled crowd as Tony started to walk up to the microphone. "I've got to go to work," he whispered to the Hardys. "Talk to me later."

As the group behind the rock star began to tune up, Frank and Joe walked to the side of the stage. They spotted Callie with a pretty, worried-looking young woman in her early twenties, and went to join them.

"Frank, this is Leslie Johnston," Callie introduced the stranger.

"It's nice to meet you face to face," Frank said.

"We may have something for you," Callie went on. "We've been over at the wrecking yard where they've got what's left of the car."

Leslie Johnston rummaged in her purse, her eyes filling with tears. "It doesn't make sense," she said. "The car was all twisted up. All I could think of was Dick inside it —"

"He couldn't have been, Mrs. Johnston," Frank said gently. "There's no way."

The woman pulled a wrinkled, torn piece of paper from her purse and handed it to Joe.

"This was on the floor of the car," Callie explained. "I don't know if it means anything."

Joe took the scrap of paper. "It looks like part of a letter on Dick Johnston's stationery."

Frank read over his shoulder. "Dear Mr. —

something or other. There's only part of the first letter, and it looks like an F with the horizontal line on top missing. Fry, maybe?"

Joe nodded. "Could be any number of letters, an E for instance, with the bottom line obliterated also." He sighed and went on, "— terribly worried about — at certain frequencies could — especially between B-flat and — dangerous that I won't — ston."

"Ston!" Frank exclaimed. "That's the last part of his name." He turned to his brother. "Joe, this is the first piece of evidence we've found. At least we know he was worried about something. Something dangerous!"

"But what?" Joe asked. "We need the rest of the letter."

"Mrs. Johnston," Frank said, "this is a carbon. Where was it typed?"

"At the shop. We don't have a typewriter at home."

"You think it's important?" Callie asked.

"It could be," Joe said. He turned to Leslie. "We must see if there's another copy at your husband's office. Would you take us there?"

"I'd rather stay here."

"What can you do here?" Frank questioned.

"Dick was excited about Tony's using his new sound system," the woman replied. "He'll show up. I just know he'll show up if he's physically able to."

"Of course. Is his office open?"

"I'll give you the key." Leslie Johnston rummaged in her purse again, then handed Frank a ring of keys. None of them noticed Carl Fry, who watched them closely from a distance.

Frank and Joe would go to Johnston's Sound System, Ltd., while Leslie and Callie would wait at the stadium. They arrived at the small industrial building, which was laid out as a laboratory-shop combination. In the main room stood various benches with electronic gear and at the rear was Dick Johnston's private office. The Hardy boys went inside. It contained a desk with a typewriter and several file cabinets. At the far wall was a closet.

Frank and Joe went straight to the file cabinets.

"What time is it?" Joe asked.

"Just after five," Frank replied.

"We'll have to hurry to get to the concert in time," Joe warned.

"Sooner we start, sooner we finish."

They each opened the top drawer of a different cabinet and thumbed through the papers. Precious time passed. As it got darker, Frank turned the light on and they continued working.

Suddenly Joe heard a click at the front entrance. "Frank," he said, "the light! We have company."

Quickly Frank flipped the switch and both boys groped in the darkness for the closet door.

"Can you see?" Frank whispered, as footsteps approached.

"No, but he's heading this way!"

Frank found the doorknob and realized the closet was locked. He pulled the ring of keys that Leslie Johnston had given him out of his pocket and fumbled nervously for one that would open the door. He tried one, but it did not fit. He tried another. The footsteps came closer, and the boys felt knots in their stomachs. Frank's hands shook as he tried one more key. It fit!

Quickly the boys unlocked the door and hid in the closet. Seconds later a man entered the office. He wore gloves and carried a two-gallon can of gasoline. Silently he walked to the telephone, shining a flashlight in front of him, and dialed a number. Frank and Joe could barely hear his muffled voice.

"The van's out front, but there's no sign of them," the man said.

"Who is it?" Joe whispered. "Haskell?"

"I don't know," Frank replied. "Shh."

"Don't worry," the intruder went on. "They'll never get a chance to read it. When that high C-sharp hits the speaker, it'll be bye-bye Bird."

"Holy —" Joe began, but his brother clamped a hand over his mouth.

"Now relax," they heard the intruder say. "Enjoy the show. You won't see another one like it for a long time."

Frank and Joe heard a click as the man replaced the phone in the cradle. Then he went to a file cabinet and began to pull papers out of the drawers, scattering them all over the floor. Finally he tipped over the whole cabinet. It hit the closet door as it fell.

The boys stared at each other in alarm. Frank tried to open the closet door but it would not budge. "Joe, it locks from the outside!" he said in a hoarse whisper. "We can't get out!"

They heard the intruder continue to dismantle the office. Suddenly his hand struck a match. Flames leaped up, and as they started to spread, he quickly ran out of the office, his footsteps echoing in the distance.

Frank and Joe pounded helplessly on the door. Both realized that the man had set a fire when they saw the flickering flames through a crack in the door. They pounded and pounded, but to no avail.

"No good," Joe panted. "We'll have to wait until the fire weakens it." He coughed.

"Too late," Frank sputtered and coughed, too. "By then we'll suffocate." He kneeled down and examined the floor, while Joe rummaged around on shelves at the rear of the closet.

"What've you got?" Frank asked.

"Power tools, I think, for all the good they'll do us."

"Think positive!" Frank encouraged his brother.

"I'm thinking positive. It's the circumstances that are negative."

"Wait a minute. Those tools might help. The wiring for the building must run along this back wall. If we can get a piece of paneling off —"

"Maybe we can tap into one of the wires!" Joe completed the sentence.

"I like the way you think."

Both kneeled down and felt the back of the closet.

"Got your knife?" Joe asked.

"Yeah. First the molding —" Frank coughed violently while Joe worked the knife into the crack between the molding and the wall. Wood splintered as the boys made progress and finally broke through to the electrical line.

"It's here, but it's in conduit," Frank said.

"Yank it out and we'll flex it till it breaks," Joe advised.

"Okay. See if there's a quarter-inch drill and a jigsaw."

As the flames spread in the office, a black cloud of smoke billowed into the closet from underneath the door. The boys tried to stop it by closing the crack with some rags they found, then worked feverishly to connect the drill.

"Here goes," Frank said. "Let's hope the fire hasn't eaten through the electrical system."

"That's what I've always admired about you, older brother," Joe said. "Your sense of humor."

Frank pushed the button of the drill and it started to whirr. Quickly he cut through the wood near the lock.

"Hallelujah!" Joe coughed again.

"Give me the saw!" Frank sputtered.

"Coming up."

Both boys coughed again. The heat became intense and they gasped for air. Frank sawed a circle around the bolt, and when he was finished, the cut-out piece popped out of the door with a clunk.

"Ready — now!" Joe cried.

The boys threw their bodies against the door. It flew open and they rushed out, holding their arms in front of their faces to protect themselves from the leaping flames.

As they ran through the office, they heard the sound of a fire engine and by the time they bolted through the front entrance, the fire chief hurried toward them.

"You boys all right?" he asked, staring at their blackened faces and arms.

"We're fine, Chief," Frank replied. He was still coughing. "Can't stop to talk to you now."

They reached the van, jumped in, and pulled away with screeching tires.

While Frank concentrated on driving, Joe picked up their C.B. radio. "Breaker, breaker, this is an emergency. Police department —"

"Police department," came the reply.

"This is Joe Hardy. Patch me through to either Chief Collig or Fenton Hardy at the stadium right away. It's urgent!"

"Patrolman Roberts," said a voice.

"I've got to speak to Chief Collig —"

"Who *is* this?"

"Joe Hardy. I've got to speak to Chief Collig or my father. It's urgent!"

"All right. I'll get the chief."

"Wait a minute!" Joe added. "Don't leave the phone. You've got to stop the performance. There's a bomb wired to — hello? Hello?" Joe sighed in frustration. "He's put the phone down."

Desperately he tried to get through again while Frank drove with fierce concentration, taking curves on two wheels.

"Operator, this is a matter of life and death!" Joe shouted into the microphone.

"I'm sorry, sir, but that line is busy," the operator replied.

"Forget it, Joe," Frank said. "We'll have to get there ourselves."

"I'll keep the line open," Joe said. "It's Tony Bird they're after."

"Who're they?" Frank asked.

"Haskell? He could be our firebug."

"But why? What's his connection with Tony or Fry?"

95

"When he hits C-sharp," Joe repeated the strange message, "it's all over, bye-bye Tony. What's going to happen?"

"Didn't sound as though he was going to lose his voice, did it?" Frank muttered.

"Yes, it did. Along with his life."

Frank shot through the stadium entrance and screeched to a halt. Instantly, the boys leaped out of the van. They heard applause and cheers of the audience at the end of one of Tony's numbers.

"He's still okay," Frank said as they rushed up the pedestrian path toward the main entrance. The turnstile area was deserted except for a ticket-taker in a blue blazer who strolled aimlessly back and forth. Another song began. It was *Games,* an all-time favorite.

"Hey, slow down!" the ticket-taker called out. "You can't —"

Frank and Joe did not stop to explain. They vaulted the turnstiles like hurdles, ran inside, and hurried down the main aisle. Yelling and gesticulating wildly, they tried to attract Tony Bird's attention, but the music drowned them out until they were more than halfway to the stage.

Even then Tony and his group were oblivious to the disturbance and went right on playing. Chief Collig, however, had noticed the boys from the other side of the huge theater, where he was positioned. He had been informed by Patrolman Roberts that Joe Hardy wanted to speak to him, but had not taken the message seriously. Now, with a gesture of despair, he scooted down another aisle toward the stage.

Callie and Leslie Johnston, too, had noticed the two soot-blackened figures and turned in their seats, a puzzled look on their faces. They saw Fenton Hardy and several security guards converging on the boys. Two guards attempted to stop them, but their momentum was too great. After a brief tussle Frank and Joe broke free and ran.

A uniformed policeman headed them off and collared Frank. Joe, however, managed to leap onto the stage. In a flash, he grabbed Tony Bird's guitar and jerked the cord out of the speaker. Tony's mouth fell open in utter amazement, and the musicians stopped playing, gaping at the panting boy.

A deadly silence fell over the audience. They watched Fenton Hardy jump up on the stage, followed by Frank, who had been released by the policeman on his father's orders.

"What the devil is going on?" Mr. Hardy thundered when they reached Joe.

"There's a bomb — something — wired up in the speaker!" Joe sputtered.

"What?"

"It was timed to go off with the music," Frank explained.

Just then Carl Fry emerged from offstage. He was livid with rage. "I hope you've got an explanation for this, Hardy!" he hissed.

"They say there's a bomb in that speaker," the detective said.

Chief Collig, who had joined the group, looked tense. "On the off chance that they're right, I'm going to evacuate this place," he decided, striding over to the microphone. He began to address the audience, but the crowd drowned him out with boos and catcalls.

Meanwhile, Carl Fry shook his head in disbelief. "A bomb? Don't be ridiculous." He went to the speaker and ripped off the netting. "Look for yourself. There's nothing there!"

Fenton Hardy stared at his mortified sons. The audience stamped and clapped; and the catcalls became louder and louder. Finally the band started to play again.

"Let's go!" the detective whispered to Frank and Joe. Dejected, they followed him backstage.

When the concert was over, Tony Bird joined them, dripping with perspiration. He handed his guitar to Carl Fry, who was right behind him. Before either Tony or Fenton Hardy had a chance to speak, Fry thundered, "What is the matter with you two? Are you crazy, disrupting a concert like that?"

He turned to Mr. Hardy. "I could take this as a breach of your contract!"

"Dad," Frank put in, "there's an explanation."

"I'd sure like to hear it!" Fry hissed.

"So would I," Fenton Hardy said evenly. "Chief Collig informed me that you were both in a fire tonight. The fire chief just got off the phone with him. The sound-systems building has burned to the ground."

"We found part of a letter Richard Johnston had written in his wrecked car," Frank explained. "We were looking for a carbon copy in his office when an intruder came in. We overheard his phone call while hiding in a closet — we couldn't get out when —"

"Slow down, Slow down," his father interrupted. "The silver streak doesn't travel that fast. Are you saying that someone started this fire deliberately?"

"That's right, Dad," Joe replied.

"To kill you?"

"He didn't know we were there. He was destroying evidence."

"Did you get a look at him?"

"No, but we heard his voice on the phone. He said Tony Bird would be gone — finished — when his high-C note hit the speaker. We were sure a bomb was wired into it."

Fry obviously did not believe one word. "Who would do such a thing?" he asked. "What's the motive? And what does Richard Johnston and Sound Systems have to do with it?"

"We don't know yet," Frank replied.

"Of course you don't! Because there's no connection!"

"We can prove Johnston was in Tony's plane in the last few days."

"All right," Mr. Hardy said. "We'll talk about it in the morning. But next time, be *sure* of your facts before you disrupt proceedings with such devastating effect."

"Look," Fry said. "No one's trying to kill him. He's too valuable to everyone. Besides, he's leaving for London in the morning." He walked away and Mr. Hardy put his arms around his sons' shoulders.

"Dad, we were so sure —" Frank began.

"You were wrong," his father said with a smile. "It happens, even to me." He paused a moment, then went on, "How long were you in that building while it was burning?"

"Long enough," Joe said grimly.

"I'm glad to have you here unhurt. You boys have *got* to be careful. I can't allow you to be involved in these cases unless —"

"We were just in the right place at the wrong time, Dad," Frank apologized.

"I'm sure the chief will want a full statement from you in the morning," Mr. Hardy went on. "Arson is a very serious crime."

"So is murder," Joe added.

Frank Hardy could not go to sleep that night. In the dark, he paced the floor of his room, stared out the window, and tried to find an answer to the puzzle. His glance fell on the lighted digital alarm clock. It was 5:35 A.M.

With a sigh, he went to his desk and sat down. He switched on the lamp and smoothed out the torn letter Leslie Johnston had given him. Then he took a blank sheet of paper and began to scribble various letter combinations. Suddenly his brows furrowed.

"Not F for Fry," Frank mumbled to himself. "H for Haskell. But why?"

Abruptly he jumped up. In the process he knocked down a model airplane, which had stood near the lamp. He picked it up absent-mindedly, then suddenly had an idea. He stared at the little plane, smiled triumphantly, then carefully put it back on the desk.

"The Gulfstream!" he said softly to himself. "That must be the answer!" Silently he hurried out of his room and downstairs into his father's office. He picked up the phone on Callie's desk and dialed a number.

"All Points Charter Service?" Frank said into the mouthpiece. "Sorry to bother you so early, but we've just had a breakdown on our Lear Jet, and I understand you have a Gulfstream available for charter."

There was a short pause, then Frank went on, "I see. Unavailable for six weeks. Well, for future reference, could you tell me — is it equipped for transatlantic flights? Leaving for London this morning? Thank you. We'll be in touch."

Frank put down the phone and went into his brother's room. "Come on, wake up," he whispered and shook the sleeping boy.

Joe did not open his eyes. "What time is it?"

"Ten to six. Will you wake up!"

Joe blinked. "What's the big —"

"Tony Bird is flying to London this morning on the Gulfstream."

"I know. He told us. I hope he has a good flight." Joe pulled the pillow over his head, but Frank yanked it away and dragged off his brother's covers.

"The letter Johnston wrote — it wasn't to Fry. It was to Haskell. Warning him about something dangerous on the Gulfstream. That's what those letters meant!"

Joe sat bolt upright. "A bomb wired into the audio system of the Gulfstream!" he cried out. "We've got to tell Dad!"

"And be wrong again? We're going to check it out ourselves. Come on!"

Quickly the boys put on their clothes and got into the van. Frank took the wheel. Dawn had just broken and he put on the lights before taking off.

"Haskell set the fire," Joe surmised, "because he

was afraid there were copies of Johnston's letter."

"Which Johnston sent to him when he figured out there was something dangerous about the audio system he designed for the Gulfstream."

Joe nodded. "That's why Johnston went to Eastwick on Friday, to follow up the letter."

"And Haskell grabbed him before he could warn Tony Bird."

"What Haskell said on the phone — 'when he hits that high-C sharp it's good-by to Tony Bird,' — he meant on the tape system of the airplane."

"He must have been talking to Fry," Frank said. "Had to be. Fry wants Tony dead. Probably has something to do with those investments. Maybe he's robbing him blind."

"You know, I've suddenly got a pretty good idea where Richard Johnston is," Joe declared.

"So do I. Two nights ago, we were probably standing on top of him!"

Meanwhile, Tony Bird and his musicians had arrived at Eastwick Field. The rock star and one of his band members wore pilot's jump suits and were checking the plane before take-off.

Carl Fry and Haskell drove up, and Tony went out through the front hatch to meet them.

His agent handed him a briefcase. "Here it is, just as I promised."

Tony took the briefcase. "Sure you won't change your mind and come along? We could go over it together, in case I have any questions."

104

Fry shook his head. "Tony, you're a great singer, but I'll fly with people who do it full time."

Tony shrugged and turned to Haskell. "You got the bugs out of the in-flight audio system?"

"All set," Haskell replied.

"You know the Hardy boys proved Richard Johnston was in this plane," Tony remarked.

"Then he broke in for some reason," Haskell said. "I never saw him." He smiled. "Have a good flight."

Tony hesitated, then shook hands with Haskell and Fry before climbing up the gangway again.

When he disappeared into the hatch, Fry called after him, "I'll see you in London tomorrow!"

Haskell wheeled away the stair unit and Tony shut the hatch. The Gulfstream's engines were revved up and the little plane trembled with power.

Lou Haskell, who was on duty as air-traffic controller that morning, went to the tower with Fry. He sat down at the radio, while Tony's manager looked out the window.

"Eastwick Tower to Gulfstream five-seven-bravo," Haskell said into the microphone. "You're cleared for takeoff. Check in when you reach cruising altitude."

"That's a roger," Tony replied. "Out."

Just then Frank and Joe drove up to the hangar. They noticed three police cars parked in the area, with uniformed officers watching the Gulfstream maneuvering for takeoff. Chief Collig was among them.

"Do you see what I see?" Frank asked Joe.

"How did they get here so fast?"

"I don't know, but they're not making one move to stop that plane from taking off!" Frank brought the van to a screeching stop. The boys jumped out, and ran up to Chief Collig.

"Chief, you've got to prevent that jet from taking off!" Frank called out.

"I don't believe it!" Collig said. "I suppose you're going to tell me there's a bomb wired into the audio system of the Gulfstream now."

"Yes, there is!" Joe cried. "And Richard Johnston is somewhere aboard, probably in the cargo hold."

Collig looked annoyed. "Let me tell you boys something. You're not the only detectives in the area practicing protective police work. I was already ahead of you. We searched that airplane with a fine-tooth comb and found absolutely *nothing*. No explosives, no tampering with the controls, no cross wiring, zero!"

"But that's impossible!" Frank exclaimed.

"What about Johnston?" Joe added.

"You think my men would overlook him? There's no one in that plane who shouldn't be there, alive or dead!"

"Haskell didn't load anything on at the last moment?" Joe asked. "After you searched?"

"No, there's nothing on that plane but instruments and reserve fuel for the overseas flight."

Frank and Joe turned away from the police chief, not knowing what to do next. They saw the

Flight to Nowhere

Gulfstream taxiing slowly onto the runway.

"When do you act on instincts?" Frank ventured.

"When they're all you've got left," Joe replied.

"We've got to stop that plane!"

"What if we're wrong?"

"We're talking about Tony's life!"

Without further hesitation, the boys ran to their van.

"Where are you going?" Chief Collig called after them. "You two come back here. I want to —"

His voice trailed off as the boys slammed the door and started the engine. The van roared down the runway at top speed. Collig stood helpless as it moved alongside the jet with no more than a few feet between them.

Haskell and Fry stared out the tower window in utter astonishment.

"Who is that?" Haskell exploded.

"Those Hardy boys," Fry replied.

"Let's get down there!"

When they emerged from the tower, the van was slightly ahead of the jet.

"Hold on!" Frank told his brother.

"I have a choice?"

Frank did not reply. Instead, he pulled the wheel sharply to the right and swung the van in front of the jet!

To avoid a head-on collision, the Gulfstream veered off to the side, its tail swinging around and missing the van by scant inches. Finally both came to a screeching halt.

Police cars drove up with their sirens blaring. The hatch opened and Tony Bird climbed out. He jumped down as Frank and Joe emerged from the van. Chief Collig, his policemen, Carl Fry, and Lou Haskell appeared on the scene seconds later.

"What's going on now?" Tony asked the young detectives.

"You're carrying reserve fuel because you're flying overseas," Frank said. "What would happen over the ocean if you went off course?"

"Why should we go off course?" Tony was puzzled. "We've got all the latest navigational instruments."

"So do commercial airlines," Frank said. "But they have warning cards that passengers can't operate FM radios on board because they interfere with the equipment."

"Richard Johnston's new stereo system," Joe added.

"Right," Frank said. "He'd discovered it could be a deadly hazard that could put the plane hundreds of miles off course out over the Atlantic."

"But we're carrying plenty of reserve fuel," Tony objected.

"What if you aren't?"

"This is ludicrous!" Lou Haskell was extremely annoyed.

"Check it out," Frank advised. "Check that drum tank in the hold. That's all we ask."

Chief Collig held up his hand. "Let's check it," he said and motioned to two mechanics in overalls who had joined the spectators around the group.

They opened the hold and climbed inside, followed by the police chief. Lou Haskell and Carl Fry seemed frozen to the spot where they were, and watched as if mesmerized.

Suddenly Chief Collig reappeared at the opening. When the two men saw his grim face, they turned and attempted to run, but the chief pulled his gun and shouted a clipped warning. Haskell and Fry were trapped!

The next moment the two mechanics struggled out of the hold with a third man. They pulled him gently and removed the tape that had been pasted over his mouth. The man looked weak and breathed shallowly. "Thank God," he said softly.

He was Richard Johnston!

"Get him to a hospital!" Chief Collig ordered.

While Haskell and Fry were handcuffed and led away, an ambulance drove up and Richard Johnston was taken to the nearest medical center for a checkup. Luckily he had not suffered any injuries and was released two hours later. A police officer drove him back to the airport, where a group had gathered in the hangar to discuss the latest developments. It included Fenton Hardy, his sons, Tony Bird, and Chief Collig.

"Fry admitted that he was in partnership with Haskell," Frank said. "They used your money, Tony, to buy the Gulfstream."

"Then, to rub salt into the wound, they overcharged you every time you chartered," Joe added.

"I'll probably find more evidence of embezzlement in my other investments," Tony said sadly. "I'd had some inkling of what was going on. That's why I told Carl I wanted to review all of my holdings."

"He had to prevent that," Fenton Hardy said.

"When I checked the audio system for the Gulfstream," Richard Johnston said, "I found that Haskell had added a high-frequency circuit. I told him to take it out because it was dangerous. That was when he grabbed me."

"When someone saves your life," Tony said quietly, "words aren't easy to find. What can I do for you guys?"

Frank and Joe shrugged and their father said

with a smile, "Invite them to your next concert."

"I'll be in London."

The boys grinned at Mr. Hardy. "A deal's a deal, Dad," Joe pointed out.

"It won't take us long to get our things out of the van," Frank added.

Fenton Hardy hesitated, then threw up his hands in resignation. "I doubt that London knows what's about to hit it —"